This book belongs to

....

For Grandpa Frank, who's adventuring in space for all of us.

Gramps and Me in the Galaxy

First Edition, 2020

Published by Big Agua Press.
City of Publication: Los Angeles, CA
For information contact: info@bigagua.com
ISBN: 978-1-952122-00-2
Library of Congress Control Number: 2020914139

GRAMPS & ME IN THE GALAXY

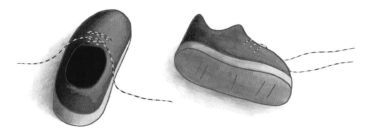

WRITTEN BY ANNA LAMSON
ILLUSTRATED BY DAVID STEDMOND

My Grandpa said he'd try to teach me everything he knows,
like how to use an oatmeal spoon to build men out of snow,

and how to ride a rhino, and how to speak Chinese,
and how to wrestle elephants by tickling their knees.

A week or two ago, my Gramps was aired on TV news.
He had captured seven monkey thieves for stealing children's shoes.
Then he threw them in a barrel, and they sang a crazy song...

about spotted purple reindeer
who danced and played ping pong.

Our town threw Gramps a party, way out in outer space.
He invited me to come along to hold his huge briefcase.
Everything was going fine. We soared among the stars.
All was perfect as a pickle 'til we met the King of Mars!

The king was tall and gray and wore antennae that could hum.
His eyes were drooped and dreary, his expression rather glum.
"Help me, please! It's coming!" the king shouted in dismay.
"It's taking over Neptune and it's coming right this way!"

We stopped our celebration and Gramps comforted the king
and gave him bottled water and a single onion ring.
"Please HELP! This MONSTROUS creature wants to rule the galaxy!
You must help me save the universe and do it valiantly!"

So we packed up all the stars and as I tipped my party hat,
the king offered us his army and his Kung Fu-fighting cat.
Grandpa kindly shook his head. We felt we'd had enough...
of stars, pink party favors, and our bad-guy-fighting stuff.

We jumped into our sailboat and we took off into flight,
passing seven swimming beets...and a tulip with stage fright!

Farther up the way we met a goat on Saturn's rings,
who warned us we must hurry, or the monster would sprout wings!

"A monster sprouting wings?" I asked, not knowing what to think.
The goat raised both his eyebrows high while sipping on squid ink.
"Not just ordinary wings," said Goat, "they flap in such a flurry.
He uses them to capture men to feed to his fish, Murray."

I looked at Gramps in awe and saw him wink with a sly grin.
He couldn't REALLY think there was a way for us to win?!

I sat nervously just thinking that this monstrous, ugly creature must surely have three heads. I bet one ate his music teacher!

Quicker than an ambulance and meaner than raccoons, he probably eats toenails with sharp, broken plastic spoons!

He'd be at least one mile tall with thirty-seven horns, have scum between his teeth, with little bits of moldy corn.

I bet he's got ten arms that stretch much longer than my street, and a bald spot on one head, and maybe rattlesnakes for feet!

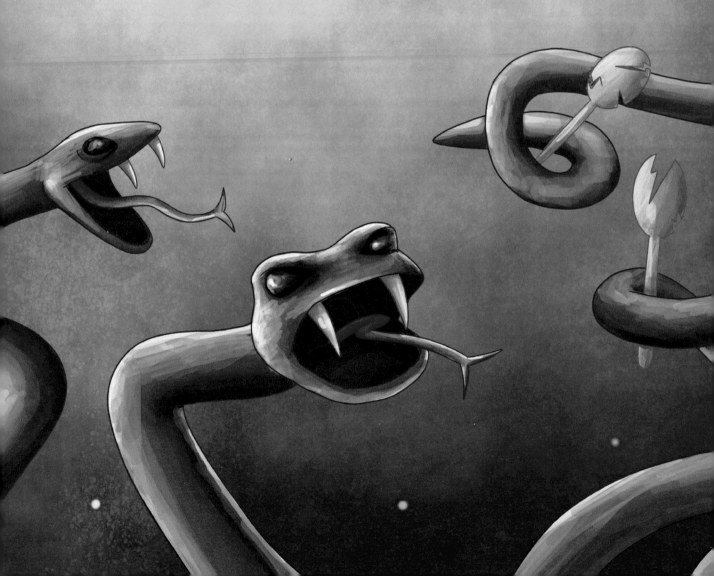

I shuddered as I thought about this monster drawing near,
but Grandpa leaned back calmly, relaxing with no fear.
What bravery! "OK," I thought, "I'm safe by Grandpa's side."
But then we noticed something strange that halted our smooth ride!

I looked where Gramps was pointing, and there sitting on Neptune
was a pink and yellow hippo holding onto a balloon!
She wasn't all that tall and her big teeth were awfully green.
She really looked quite goofy and her name tag read "Francine."

So was this the big, mean monster? A two-tone portly hippo?
No one was prepared for this. We'd better get a grippo!
This was not a monster! It was only odd Francine,
disrupting the whole universe while making quite a scene.

Poor Francine sat there crying...
She was sobbing!
She was shaking!
And poor Neptune!

It was flooding!

It was sinking!

IT WAS **QUAKING!**

"Charge!" I shouted and I ran, attacking with our stars,
but Grandpa simply caught them in his big transparent jars.

Confused, I watched as Gramps approached poor Fran on tippy toes
to soothe the troubled hippo with bananas and a rose.

Francine refused each offering and rubbed her teary eyes
as Gramps continued searching through his briefcase of supplies.

The hippo whimpered loudly, wanting none of Grandpa's things,
and explained why she was crying – she had lost her
striped shoestrings!

As Grandpa winced and wiggled, these must have been my cues,
'cause looking down I saw the perfect answer in my shoes!

"Look at this!" I shouted as I ran to Grandpa quick.
I untied both my shoes and simply flung them with a kick.
I raced to the sad hippo with my laces and I said,
"Mine have stripes like yours! They go really well with red!"

The hippo stopped her sobbing as she shouted out, "THANK YOU!"
Neptune stopped its quaking, so it's now as good as new!

King Mars gave us a trophy and the solar system cheered!
Then last night on the TV news, both Gramps and I appeared.

This time they said, "Let's celebrate deep beneath the sea!"
Perhaps this is the start of a new trip for Gramps and me!

About the Author

Anna Lamson is a Los Angeles based super mommy with a big passion for writing and a growing love for gardening. She's a satisfactory cook, but Asian cuisine is her specialty and she would serve every dish with rice if she could! Working and mommying full-time keep her busy, but she makes sure to find time to follow her passion. She hopes you enjoyed her first book!

About the Illustrator

David Stedmond is an Ireland-based illustrator and designer with a BA in graphic design. He works both in traditional and digital media. David's primary focus is illustration for children's literature. Other interests include portrait drawing, landscape painting, and music composition.

Made in the USA
Las Vegas, NV
10 December 2020

12660491R00026